Pony in Disguise

www.**kidsatrandomhouse**.co.uk
www.**rbooks**.co.uk

For fun, games and lots, lots more visit
www.**katiesperfectponies**.co.uk

PONY IN DISGUISE
A BANTAM BOOK 978 0 553 82084 3

First published in Great Britain by Bantam,
an imprint of Random House Children's Books
A Random House Group Company

This edition published 2008

1 3 5 7 9 10 8 6 4 2

The Random House Group Limited makes every effort to ensure that the papers used
in its books are made from trees that have been legally sourced from well-managed
and credibly certified forests. Our paper procurement policy can be found at:
www.randomhouse.co.uk/paper.htm

Set in 14/21pt Bembo MT Schoolbook

Bantam Books are published by Random House Children's Books,
61–63 Uxbridge Road, London W5 5SA

www.**kidsatrandomhouse**.co.uk
www.**rbooks**.co.uk

Addresses for companies within The Random House Group Limited
can be found at: www.randomhouse.co.uk/offices.htm

THE RANDOM HOUSE GROUP Limited Reg. No. 954009
A CIP catalogue record for this book is available from the British Library.

Printed in the UK by CPI Bookmarque, Croydon, CR0 4TD

Katie Price's Perfect Ponies

Pony in Disguise

Illustrated by Dynamo Design

Bantam Books

Vicki's Riding School

Vicki

Jess and Rose

Cara and Taffy

Amber and Stella

Sam and Beanz

Mel and Candy

Henrietta and President

Darcy and Duke

Chapter One

Sam emptied a packet of chocolate eggs into
the baskets that lay in front of her on the
tack-room table and grinned.
With the bright yellow
and green Eastery
ribbons she'd tied
onto them, they
looked wicked! She
was really excited.
Vicki – the owner
of Sam's riding school
– had organized an Easter
egg competition at the stables and
Sam and her friends were all taking part.

Sam picked up the first two baskets and carried them into the yard. Her best friends, Jess, Amber, Mel, Cara and Darcy, were there already, chatting in the sunshine. They were *all* members of Vicki's Riding School and were as pony-mad as Sam. But in every other way they were totally different!

Jess had thick brown hair and lovely green eyes. She was lively and confident. Jess's best friend was Amber – a beautiful Asian girl with warm, deep brown eyes. Amber was very clever and always sensitive to the ponies' needs. Then there was Mel. She was a real tomboy and already a good show-jumper. Sam got scared when Mel was feeling competitive! Mel's best friend was Cara. She was the complete opposite – really shy and quiet and she worried *a lot*. Sam's mum was always saying that she wished some of Cara would rub off on Sam. "Maybe one day," Sam always answered cheekily, while her

brother Alfie laughed out loud. Finally there
was Darcy. She was a lot of fun and had a
long plait that dangled right the way down
her back. Sam kept her own messy ginger
hair really short – she didn't know how
Darcy could be bothered to plait her waist-
length hair every day.

Of all the girls, only Darcy owned her
pony – Duke, a stunning dark bay show-
jumper who was kept in livery at Vicki's
stables. Darcy looked after him as much as
she could and hardly ever asked the
yard girls to do her
chores for her.

The others owed *their* ponies to Vicki.
Because they'd worked so hard sweeping
the yard and mucking out the stables, Vicki
had given each of them their own pony to
look after. Sam had Beanz, a lively skewbald
New Forest cross. Sam and Beanz had got
on straight away. When she and her mum
had gone to look round the stables that first
time, Vicki had shown them the yard ponies,
stopping to chat outside Beanz's stable.
Beanz had started to neigh and nudge Vicki's
tummy. Sam wondered what he was doing,
but Vicki knew straight
away!

"Oh, no! Greedy boy," she said sternly. She turned to Sam and her mum to explain. "Beanz is always the first to sniff out the mints I carry in my pocket!" she laughed.

Sam knew then that they'd get on brilliantly! And they had done ever since. He was hard work and *very* frisky. Sam had to keep him calm when they were at big events as he quickly got over-excited. But they totally trusted each other now and made a great team.

Sam thought how clever Vicki was to have matched them all up so well to their ponies. Jess had pretty, lively Rose – a silvery grey Connemara; Amber had Stella – a gentle, patient black Highland pony with a white blaze; spirited, stubborn Candy – a beautiful Arab – belonged to fiery Mel, and Cara had sturdy, laid-back Taffy – a creamy blonde palomino Welsh. All of them worked brilliantly together, Sam mused.

Darcy snapped her out of her daydream. "What are you grinning to yourself about?" she asked.

"Ha, ha!" Sam laughed. "I bet I look like a right idiot. But" – she chucked some of the spare Easter ribbon at Darcy – "I was thinking how lucky we all are."

"We definitely are," Cara agreed, coming over and putting her arm round Sam.

Vicki came by, leading Carol, a cheeky young cream-coloured Shetland – the newest pony at the stables. She smiled at the girls, and at Sam's egg baskets. "They look great, Sam. Good one!"

The others, who had come over to join them, all agreed.

"How come you've managed to get these baskets so neat," Mel asked, grinning at her scruffy friend, "when you're the messiest person I know?"

"Oh, don't be mean, Melly," said Cara.

"She wouldn't be our Sam if she was all tidy!"

"Don't worry, Car," Sam replied quickly, moving over to stroke Carol's soft nose. "I'd just rather get here quicker and spend more time with Beanz than sort my hair!"

Jess looked at her smiling freckly face. "We can see that, babe!" she joked, picking bits of fluff and sellotape out of her friend's red hair. "But we love you exactly the way you are."

"And it's obvious that Beanz is really loved

7

and cared for," Amber said. "Not like poor President and Cleo."

President, a spotty grey Appaloosa, and Cleo, a striking dark Arab, belonged to Henrietta Reece-Thomas and her best friend, Camilla Worthington. They were girls who, like Darcy, kept their ponies at livery with Vicki. But that was the only way in which they were anything like Darcy! They were spoiled and mean and caused lots of problems for Vicki and the girls. What annoyed Sam and the others most of all was that they didn't seem interested in their ponies, leaving whoever was on livery duty to do everything for them.

Mel shook her head angrily. "I don't know why it still bothers me — I mean, we know what they're like."

Vicki looked at her watch and interrupted the girls. "Our volunteers will start arriving in half an hour, girls, and I want to make sure everything's perfect before they get here."

Sam looked at Vicki. She was holding tightly onto Carol's lead rope and running her other hand through her long dark hair as if she was well stressed. Sam wasn't surprised. Vicki was in training with her beautiful Irish-cross thoroughbred, Jelly, *and* still running the stables. A couple of years ago, when Sam was new to the school, Vicki and Jelly had qualified for Badminton — a famous three-day event — but since then Vicki had taken a break from competing so she could concentrate on the stables. Now she wanted to get back into it, and in a couple of weeks she was taking part in an amateur jumping competition to see if she was ready to start again seriously. Sam hoped she was – she'd love Vicki to win something.

"Sam," Vicki said now, "will you get the rest of those baskets from the tack room so that Susie and I can give them to the stewards when they arrive?"

"I'm gonna be well proud when everybody from the other schools arrives," Sam announced.

Susie – Vicki's eighteen-year-old assistant – smiled at her.

"Well," said Vicki, "I hope you know that I'll be proud of you lot too – as always. I couldn't have got ready for today *and* kept training without your help."

"I hope you win, Vicki!" Mel shouted excitedly.

Vicki crossed her fingers. "Me too!"

"I wish we could come and watch," Sam said. She'd love to see Vicki all dressed up on Jelly. "I bet it'd be brilliant."

"Oh, it's quite a drive from here, Sam, I—" Vicki began, but she stopped suddenly as she realized what Carol was up to.

The naughty Shetland had her head in one of Sam's beautiful baskets and was stuffing her face with chocolates!

The girls laughed out loud. Carol had eaten nearly all the Easter eggs *and* the wrappers too!

Vicki laughed. "No other pony I've ever met has liked chocolate," she said, taking the basket out of Carol's reach.

"Oh, no," groaned Cara. "Your beautiful basket, Sammy."

"Sorry, Sam," Vicki said. "Can you get another one sorted? I'll take this naughty pony over to the meadow where she'll be well out of the way!" And she led Carol away, leaving the girls still giggling.

Chapter Two

Half an hour later, the girls had redone the basket Carol had scoffed and were tacking up their ponies ready for the competition. They chatted happily in the spring sunshine.

"I'm well excited about today." Amber grinned, tying a yellow Easter ribbon round Stella's browband.

"Me too," Sam added. "But I'm glad Beanz doesn't like chocolate eggs," she laughed as she struggled to do up his girth. "He's already got fatter over the winter!"

"Oh, he'll get skinny again," Jess said. "Today will do him good for a start."

"I'm getting really nervous about it now,"

Cara said quietly.

Not quietly enough! At that moment, Henrietta Reece-Thomas strode into the yard. "You're so pathetic!" she sneered. "How hard can it be? We're only riding round the fields and answering some stupid questions and stuff – it'll be totally boring. I suppose we'll get some chocolate at least."

"Shut up, Henrietta!" shouted Mel. "Today's gonna be brilliant."

"Oh, you're just sucking up to Vicki like always," the livery girl answered snidely.

"Now who's pathetic?" Sam asked her. "The Easter egg course is s'posed to be fun for us all."

"Well, don't get too excited. Milly and I are *bound* to come first. Camilla's mum is one of the stewards – I'm sure she'll make sure the best people win."

"You can't cheat!" gasped Mel.

"Don't accuse me of cheating," Henrietta

snapped. "I just said that the *best people* should win. And I'm sure they will."

"Well, it doesn't matter anyway — Vicki's not stupid; if you get help from Camilla's mum, I'm sure she'll figure it out," Jess told her.

Henrietta looked down her nose at the girls and started to walk away. But then she stopped and turned back. "Oh, by the way, Camilla's had to go and meet her mother and I'm going to join them for a picnic brunch before we start. Finish tacking up President and Cleopatra for when we get back," she ordered.

Sam went as red as her hair with anger! "How dare—" she started.

But Henrietta interrupted her. "What's your problem? You're stable hands. It's what you're supposed to do.

15

We'll expect the ponies to be ready in half an hour," and with that she stormed off.

Mel was fuming. "What an idiot!" she shouted.

Jess and Amber were on livery duty that week; they finished off their ponies quickly so that they could see to President and Cleopatra.

"I'll come too," Cara offered kindly. "If there's three of us we'll get them done faster."

Sam and Mel looked at each other when the others had left. Sam adjusted Beanz's bridle. "I just can't believe that there are real girls our age who behave like that," she said, shaking her head.

Mel agreed. "No way do they deserve those ponies—" she started, but then stopped as she spotted Vicki leading a group of people across the yard; they were holding ribbons and Sam's egg baskets!

"Gosh!" she laughed. "Vicki looks like the Pied Piper of Hamelin! I so didn't realize there'd be this many people!"

"I know," Sam answered. "Good job Cara's not here to see! She'd totally freak!"

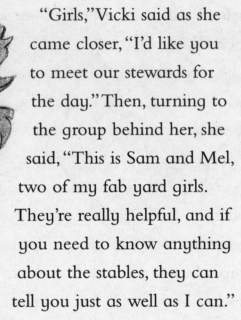

"Girls," Vicki said as she came closer, "I'd like you to meet our stewards for the day." Then, turning to the group behind her, she said, "This is Sam and Mel, two of my fab yard girls. They're really helpful, and if you need to know anything about the stables, they can tell you just as well as I can."

Both girls blushed bright red.

A few of the stewards — including Camilla's mum — wandered off. Some were checking details with each other and looking around the yard. Vicki's school was lucky because it had lots of fields and tracks, so the Easter egg trail could go all round the stables.

Vicki introduced the lady standing next to her. "Sam, Mel," she said. "This is my friend Lucy. She runs the West Farm Riding School."

Lucy was very different from Vicki, who looked like a model. Lucy was short and stocky and Sam could tell that she was fit and strong. There were a couple of young women and a man with her too. "Lucy's school's much bigger than ours so she has lots of volunteers," Vicki told them. "She's brought a few of them along to help us today. Are you all OK with what you're doing and where?" she asked them.

The stewards nodded and smiled.

"Great!" she exclaimed. "Well, if everyone's OK, then I'm going to collect Flora and take her over to the meadow to join Carol."

Sam and Mel nodded, but Lucy's volunteers looked puzzled.

"Two of my ponies aren't being used today. They've not really built up any fitness since the winter, so the meadow's the best place for them!" Vicki explained. "I know they'd much rather be there than trudging round a course with one of the Saturday kids on top of them!"

As she strode off, one of the stewards, a sandy-haired man, came over to Beanz's stable to talk to the girls. "How do you do?"

He was smiling, but Sam noticed that he didn't look at her when he spoke. His eyes were darting about all over the place, which made her uncomfortable – though Mel answered him enthusiastically enough. Sam didn't want to show Vicki up, so she said, "Thanks so much for coming to help today – I know Vicki's really grateful."

"No problem," he answered smoothly.

"It's always interesting to see other riding schools and the different ponies they have." He reached up to pat Beanz's nose. "He's a handsome boy," he said. "Do you look after him?"

Before Sam could answer, Beanz whinnied, jerking his head away from the stranger.

"Don't worry. Beanz is the friskiest pony Vicki's got," Mel joked. "Just like his mistress!"

Sam smiled politely but inside she was angry. The man must have scared Beanz to make him react like that. He was much calmer these days and hardly ever tossed his head like that when Sam was around.

"I'm Tim, by the way," the man said. "Which of you lovely ladies is Sam and which of you is Mel?"

"I'm Mel," said Mel. "And this is Sam – you can't miss her, and if you did, you'd hear her first!"

"Well," Tim said, giving them a big smile again. "I'm sure I'll see *and* hear you on the course. Good luck!" And he walked off whistling and swinging his egg basket.

Soon everything was in place: the competitors from other schools had arrived and Vicki had gathered them all together in the yard to explain the rules of the Easter egg competition. Sam looked

down at Beanz proudly. His patchy brown
and white coat shone in the sunlight and his
tack gleamed.

"Hi, everyone!" Vicki called, across the
noise of the children and ponies in her yard.
"I'm really pleased you're all here today.
You'll work in pairs."

Sam and Darcy looked at each other and
Sam winked at her friend. They'd already
decided that they would
pair up.

"And you'll all begin at a different point on the course, somewhere around the school," Vicki continued.

"Yuck!" Sam heard Henrietta whisper to Camilla. "All these idiots on their borrowed ponies trotting round like they own the place!"

Sam looked daggers at the spiteful girls but they just ignored her.

"At each of these starting positions, there will be a different steward with a basket full of eggs. They will ask you a question. If you get the question right, there will be an egg for each of you and a little treat for your pony. The steward will point you in the right direction to carry on. Don't worry – the trail is very clearly marked out all the way round. If you don't get the question right, you still carry on, but you won't get an egg. Do you all understand so far?" The riders nodded at her, so she went on. "Now, none of the eggs or the pony treats are to be eaten until you've answered all ten questions."

"Excuse me, Vicki," Camilla interrupted. "What do we do when we get all the answers? I mean, how will Henrietta and I know we've won?"

"She's so cocky!" Darcy muttered, making Sam giggle.

Vicki raised her eyebrows but carried on calmly. "When you have visited all ten stewards, you leave the trail and make your way back here to me," she told them. "Any other questions?"

A couple of the smaller children wanted something explaining, but it didn't take Vicki long to get them sorted.

"Right!" she called. "I'm about to give you all a little bag to carry your eggs and treats in and tell you where you should go to start. Before I do, I will just say one more thing: I will not tolerate rude behaviour of any kind. Do you understand?" she said, looking directly at Henrietta and Camilla.

Henrietta tutted loudly, but nodded eventually as Vicki kept staring at her.

"OK, then!" Vicki shouted. "Have fun, be careful — and good luck!" As soon as she'd given the first pair their bags and starting point, they headed off towards the field. One by one everybody rode away, until only Sam and Darcy were left. As Vicki handed them their bags, she winked. "Come on, girls! You can do this easily!"

Chapter Three

Because Sam and Darcy were the last to leave, their starting point was the closest to the yard. They made their way over to where Susie was standing in a luminous vest.

"OK, girls." She grinned at them. "The first question should be easy . . . As well as your hat, what safety item should you always put on if you were going to be doing any jumping?"

"A back protector!" they yelled at the same time.

"Exactly!" Susie cried. "Well done! Here are your first eggs, and the treats for these guys," she said, stroking Beanz and then

Duke on their noses.

"Oh, come on, Susie," Sam teased. "Aren't you going to test us a bit more than that? We'll walk this competition if all the questions are this easy!"

"Don't get too cocky, Sam. Some of them are hard!" she warned.

The girls set off, laughing as they followed the trail round towards the fields.

"It's weird, isn't it?" Darcy said. "Because we're all riding the course separately, we don't know how anybody else is doing."

She spoke too soon! Henrietta and Camilla suddenly came thundering past. Sam had a hard time keeping Beanz under control.

"I told you this stupid competition was going to be boring," Henrietta shouted to her friend.

"What's her problem?" Darcy asked, frowning.

The girls trotted up to the next steward.
It was Camilla's mum. Sam couldn't mistake
the snooty face or the long nose!

"Oh, no!" Darcy muttered under her
breath.

"Well, I'm sure you won't get this
as quickly as my daughter did," Mrs
Worthington told them. "But here's your
next question . . . If you knock down a jump
when showjumping, how many faults do
you get?"

Sam and Darcy looked at each other.

"Vicki's told us this so many times," Darcy said. "Let me think for a minute."

"Is it three?" Sam wondered out loud. "No!" she said, remembering. "It's four! Our answer is four, Mrs Worthington."

"Hmmm," Camilla's mum said. "I have to take your first answer, and you said *three*."

Sam took a deep breath, and smiled as sweetly as she could. "I was just thinking out loud, Mrs W. Our answer is definitely four."

"No, I'm sorry—" she started.

But Darcy stepped forward. "Oh please, Mrs Worthington. Our answer is four. We're sorry we didn't make it clear that we were only thinking when Sam said *three*."

"Well," she said crossly, "I suppose I'll have to give you the benefit of the doubt . . ." And she shoved the eggs and pony treats at the girls.

Mel and Cara came up behind them.

"I see Snooty Knickers and her only friend are storming round the course spoiling it for everybody else, as usual," Mel said angrily.

Sam tried to stop her friend, pointing at Mrs Worthington, but it was too late.

"How dare you talk about my daughter and her best friend like that?" Camilla's mum snapped. "I definitely heard Vicki say something about rude behaviour, and you've definitely just been rude. I'll be sure to report you."

Mel looked furious!

"Can we have our next question please, Mrs Worthington, so we don't lose any more time?" Cara asked politely to try and smooth things over.

31

Sam and Darcy grinned at Mel and
cantered off. They got the next few questions
quickly. Darcy knew straight away that the
coronary band is at the top of a pony's hoof
and Sam knew that if a pony's field got
very wet and muddy in the winter it could
develop mud fever. And they both knew that
an eggbutt snaffle was a comfortable type
of bit, because they'd laughed their heads off
when Vicki first told them its name, and had
remembered it ever since!

As they rode up to Tim's station at the end of the far field, he grinned at them and said, "Hi, girls! It's Sam, right?"

"Yes," Sam said. "And this is Darcy." Sam felt Beanz tense and she tightened her grip on the reins, wondering why he was suddenly spooked.

"Well, Sam and Darcy," Tim asked them in a friendly voice, "can you tell me why you should check your girth before you mount your pony?"

Darcy and Sam whispered to each other, double checking the answer, then Darcy said, "So it's tight enough that the saddle won't slip."

But Tim wasn't listening — he looked like his mind was elsewhere and he didn't hear Darcy's answer.

33

"So it's tight enough that the saddle won't slip," Sam repeated loudly.

Tim jumped. "Wow! OK," he answered. "No need to shout!" But he smiled as he passed over their eggs and treats. "Good luck!" he called as they trotted off.

They answered three more questions just as quickly and got three more eggs each, when Sam spotted Jess and Amber just ahead of them on the course.

"I could kick myself!" Jess said to them crossly.

"We didn't get the answer to your mum's question," Amber explained – Sam's mum was acting as a steward too.

"So we're definitely not going to win 'cos we won't have all the eggs," Jess moaned.

"Sorry, guys," Darcy said sympathetically. "It must be a hard one if you didn't get it, Am."

Sam and Darcy made their way over to

Sam's mum.

"Hi, love!" she called. "Hi, Darcy! OK?"

"Yep, but from the look on Jess and Amber's faces, your question must be tough!" Sam grinned.

"If your pony has a little white mark between his nostrils, what is it called?" Sam's mum asked.

"A snip!" Darcy said immediately.

Sam gave her a high-five. "Darcy, that was wicked!" she said. "I would've had no idea. How did you know that?"

Darcy grinned. "Because the first horse I ever rode had one. And his name was Snip!"

"Well done, girls!" Sam's mum said. "Your egg bags look full. Are you finished?"

"Yep!" Sam told her. "We'd better get back to Vicki and see if we've won."

"Well, you definitely answered my question quickest!" Sam's mum called after them. "Good luck!"

But when Sam and Darcy reached the yard, they groaned. Henrietta and Camilla were already there, looking *very* pleased with themselves. Mel and Cara were there too – Mel looked ready to punch somebody!

"Uh-oh!" Sam laughed. "I think we should stand in the middle in case there's a fight!"

Twenty minutes later, Henrietta and Camilla had been declared the winners and were strutting round the yard showing off the massive Easter eggs they'd won. All the other riders were going off to meet their parents, but the stable girls and Darcy were staying on to do their chores.

Henrietta started to gloat straight away. "Well, I said the best people would win, and they did!"

"Henrietta, Camilla," Vicki said firmly, interrupting her. "You've done really well. Congratulations. But good horsewomen don't show off." She took a deep breath. "Now, once you've put your own ponies back in their stables, would you mind collecting Carol and Flora from the meadow and bringing them back to theirs?"

"Why can't the stable hands do it?" Henrietta asked indignantly. "Isn't that the only reason they're here?"

"No!" Vicki shouted. Sam couldn't believe
Henrietta was arguing with Vicki. "That
is *not* the only reason they're here. And I'd
appreciate it if you would do as you were
asked. Am I going to have to speak to your
parents about your future at my stables?"

Henrietta tossed her
blonde hair and
stormed off, with
Camilla close
behind.

"Idiot!" whispered Jess as she left.

"I hope you don't think you're only here as stable hands," Vicki said to them. "I couldn't cope without you girls."

They blushed shyly.

"Why don't you go and get your ponies sorted?" she suggested. "Don't tell Henrietta and Camilla but I've got a secret extra stash of Easter eggs in my office. Let's have some of those when you're finished. It's been a long morning!"

Laughing and joking, the girls led the ponies back to their stables to untack and groom them.

39

Sam wanted to see her mum off, so she kissed Beanz on the nose and untacked him quickly, before saying, "Back in a minute, babe," and running off.

When she'd walked her mum to the car and kissed her goodbye, she crossed the yard again to go and groom Beanz. "Uh-oh!" she said to herself as she saw Henrietta striding towards her with a nasty look on her face.

"Honestly," the livery girl said. "I think Vicki's losing it – that ugly little Shetland isn't even *in* the meadow."

Sam suddenly had a funny feeling in her tummy. Vicki *never* got things wrong and she'd seen her take Carol off to the meadow that morning. "What do you mean, she's not there?"

"I – mean," Henrietta said slowly, as if Sam was stupid, "she – is – not – there. Maybe one of your posse took her before I got there – probably sucking up to Vicki as usual."

Ignoring Henrietta's bitchiness, Sam rushed over to where Vicki was standing, talking to Tim. "Vicki!" she called out.

"What on earth's the matter, Sam?" Vicki looked concerned.

"Henrietta's come back without Carol," she said anxiously.

"I cannot trust those girls to do anything," Vicki snapped crossly. Then she stopped suddenly, noticing Sam's face.

"It's not like you to tell tales, though," she added softly. "What's the problem, babe?"

"Henrietta says Carol's not in the field, even though Flora's still there. I don't know who would have moved her without you knowing."

41

"I'll go and check," Vicki said, rushing over to the meadow with Sam close behind. "I'm sure I shut the gate properly. I *was* in a rush though. Oh, I hope she hasn't wandered off," she muttered to herself as she ran.

When they got to the meadow, Vicki gasped in shock. The five-bar gate was locked and Flora was still happily dozing in the sunshine. Everything looked normal . . . but Carol was nowhere to be seen.

Chapter Four

Vicki and Sam looked at each other in shock.

Tim, who had followed them to the meadow, came over to Vicki and put an arm round her. "Come on, Vicki," he said softly. "Don't panic. Ponies can't just disappear!" And he laughed.

Vicki didn't laugh. She stood there, frowning. "You're right," she said suddenly. "They can't. Sam – go and see if any of the other girls have moved Carol. I'll check whether she's already back in her stable."

"OK, Vicki," Sam answered quickly, running over to the stables, where she knew her friends would still be grooming their ponies.

When she got there, the girls were chatting. They all looked up when they heard Sam pelting towards them.

"What's up?" Amber asked, noticing Sam's anxious expression straight away.

"Carol!" Sam gasped, out of breath. "Did any of you get her from the meadow and take her back to her stable?"

"Not me," Amber answered, puzzled.

"Me neither," said Mel.

Jess and Cara shook their heads too.

"Why? What's going on, Sam?" Jess asked, dropping her hoofpick.

"She wasn't in the meadow when Henrietta went to get her, so Vicki and me went to check. Flora's still there and the gate's still locked but there's no sign of Carol!" Sam told them, getting her breath back. "I need to go and tell Vicki that you've not moved her," and she ran off again without waiting for them to answer.

The rest of the girls looked at each other.

Then Cara spoke softly. "I'm gonna see if I can help."

"Me too," said Amber, putting a dandy brush back in her shiny tack box.

"Let's all go," Jess said – organizing them as usual. "Mel, give Darcy a shout. She'll want to help. And the more of us there are, the quicker we'll find Carol."

They all set off.

"What if we don't find her? I hope she's OK," Cara whispered to Amber as they ran.

Half an hour later, all the girls had red faces and were really stressed out. They'd helped Vicki search the whole school *and* the nearby fields and there was no sign of the little cream Shetland.

They were standing in the yard outside Vicki's office and Sam thought how happy everybody had been when they'd gathered here to start the Easter competition just a few hours earlier. Now everybody was frowning, Cara was in tears and Vicki looked really worried. She kept running her hand nervously through her dark hair.

"Right," Vicki said. "That's it, I'm calling the police."

Just then, as if by magic, Mel's dad strode into the yard in his policeman's uniform. "Hello! Anybody there?" he called.

In all the panic
and fuss, Mel
had totally
forgotten
that her dad
was picking
her up so they
could go and
visit her gran!

"I've been waiting in the car for ages,"
he said, "so I just thought I'd come and see
where you'd got to . . . Is everything OK?"
he asked, noticing all the worried faces.

"I'm *so* glad to see you!" Vicki said,
relieved. "I think I need to report a robbery
. . ." and she filled him in on Carol's
mysterious disappearance.

When she'd finished, Tim spoke up: "It's
been heaving here all morning — lots of cars
and horseboxes have been in and out *and*
there's been loads of people picking kids up.

If she has been stolen, it would've been quite easy for us to miss it with everything else that was going on."

Mel's dad nodded. "I'll give the station a call and get them to send some officers over, Vicki. Don't panic, we'll find her. Now, has anything else been stolen?"

"It doesn't look like it," Vicki told him. "That's why it's so weird. Everything seems totally normal."

But things weren't normal. It was nearly an hour before the other police officers arrived. The girls hovered around nervously as a tall policeman with dark hair and a blonde

WPC got out of the car. After speaking to Mel's dad, they'd done a quick check round the meadow and Carol's stable for anything suspicious and then come back to speak to Vicki.

"She's got an ID number branded on her, I suppose?" the policeman asked.

"Not yet," Vicki said, shaking her head sadly. "I've only had her a few months. She was booked to have her freeze mark done next week – how frustrating!"

"Well, that's going to make it a bit harder," he admitted. "But never mind. Can I see her passport?"

"Course – I'll get it now," she said, running off.

When Vicki got back from her office, there were tears in her eyes. "It's not there," she cried. "I keep every pony's details and documents in my filing cabinet. Carol's folder was at the front of the drawer but it's gone!"

"Is there anywhere else it could be?" the policewoman asked softly. "Have you had it out in the last couple of days?"

"Definitely not," Vicki replied. "I see it every time I open the drawer, because it's at the front. It was definitely there yesterday."

"Was the cupboard locked? Or the office?" the policeman asked.

"I keep the filing cabinet locked, but the key's always just on the desk – nobody uses the office apart from me, and sometimes Susie. It wasn't locked today because I was in and out and the first aid kit's in there so I wanted anybody who needed it to be able to reach it easily," Vicki said sadly. "You read about this in the news all the time. But I never thought it would happen to me!"

"So you're reporting the passport missing too?"

"Yes . . ." Vicki said softly.

"OK," the policeman said, making some

notes. "Do you have the pony's registration number written anywhere else?" he asked.

"Yes, yes!" Vicki answered quickly. "I've got it with all the others in a spreadsheet on the computer in the office."

"If we can get that from you before we leave, it would be helpful. We'll start an investigation and fingerprint the door handle and key — but I'm sorry, we might not get much," he told her softly.

"Have you any idea what might have happened, officers?" Tim asked.

"Can't be sure at this stage, sir," the policewoman answered. "Just leave it to us. We'll be in touch as soon as we need something or we've got any info."

Vicki burst into tears as soon as they left. "How horrible! Poor Carol. This is all my fault!" she said, wiping her eyes. "Oh! And I've got the competition next week – that's the last thing I should be worrying about now. Maybe I should just pull out."

"No!" the girls all shouted at the same time.

"Vicki, please don't. We'll—" Sam started.

But Tim interrupted her. "Girls," he said, putting his arm round Vicki, "why don't you go home if your ponies are sorted? I'll stay for a bit and make Vicki a cup of tea."

One by one, the girls hugged Vicki goodbye, before Tim led her into the house.

"He's nice," Cara said as they went to say goodbye to their ponies. "I'm glad he's staying to look after Vicki."

"I don't like him," Sam answered stubbornly. It wasn't like her to dislike anybody – except Henrietta and Camilla, of course – but Tim annoyed her. "We hardly know him and he's bossing us around like he runs the stables."

Darcy looked surprised. "He seems OK to me. Don't you think he was just being nice because he could see how upset Vicki was about Carol?" she asked.

"Dunno," Sam replied sulkily. Then she shook her head. "Maybe we got off on the wrong foot because Beanz didn't like him. I'm just being moody because I'm sad about Carol, I guess. Sorry, guys."

Amber gave her a hug. "We're all sad, babe. How could anybody just walk in and take somebody else's pony in the middle of the day?"

"The police didn't seem very hopeful," Darcy said, puzzled.

Jess had been silent the whole time the police had been at the stables, but now she spoke up. "I heard them talking to Mel's dad when they first arrived," she said softly. "They said that in cases like this, they hardly ever find the pony . . . Poor Carol."

The girls looked at each other sadly and Cara burst into tears again. But Sam shook her head. "No, guys, we're *not* going to let that happen. It's like Tim said, *Ponies don't just disappear.* Carol must be somewhere and *we're* going to help find her!"

"Ooh! How?" Jess asked.

"Flyers, posters?" Sam suggested.

"Oh!" Darcy burst out. "My uncle works for the local paper – we'll get him to do an article on Carol."

"And we can post adverts on a couple of pony websites," Amber added. "I bet my dad could show me how."

"Brilliant!" said Sam. "Somebody must have seen something. If we do all this, I'm sure we'll find Carol."

"Let's do it!" Jess grinned.

Even Cara smiled. "Think how happy Vicki would be," she said.

Sam nodded. "Hang on, Carol, wherever you are. We're coming . . ."

Chapter Five

Sam and the girls were meeting early the next day to go through their plans and make a start on the posters and flyers. Sam got there extra-early. She wanted to spend some decent time with Beanz, as she'd rushed his grooming the day before.

After she'd tied him up outside his stable, she started to make him look as beautiful as possible. She couldn't believe how long it used to take her! Now she was much quicker, but she still liked to take her time. First she picked each foot up in turn and removed all the dirt with her hoofpick. Then, starting just behind his ears, she worked her way all over his coat with the dandy brush and then the body brush before sorting out his mane and tail. She was concentrating so hard that she didn't notice Darcy come up behind her.

"He looks gorgeous, Sam," Darcy said.

Sam smiled proudly. *She* thought that Beanz was the best pony at the stables but it was always nice to hear somebody else praise him. "Thanks, mate," she said, looking at her pony, his coat gleaming in the early morning sun. "Spending time with him really takes my mind off things."

"I know what you mean." Darcy smiled. "Talking of taking your mind off things," she went on, "I've got a surprise."

"Oooh," Sam said excitedly. "Is it something to help with the search for Carol?"

"No, 'fraid not," Darcy said. "Though I've spoken to my uncle and he's going to send a reporter round to see Vicki. But I was telling my mum about Carol and how stressed Vicki was because she's training for this event too. Mum asked if I wanted her to take me to watch when Vicki competes!"

"Wow!" Sam said. "That's wicked. Lucky you!"

"Not just lucky me," Darcy added. "I asked if she'd take you guys as well and she said she'd take as many of us as would fit in her car!"

"That's fab!" Sam cried. "Though we can't all fit in one car," she went on thoughtfully.

"Well, I wondered if maybe somebody else's mum or dad would like to take some of us too – then we could all go. I know

Jess's mum doesn't drive, but maybe there's somebody else?"

"I'm sure my mum'd be up for it!" Sam said excitedly. "She's brilliant when there's something I really, really want to do. I'll call now and ask her. Can I borrow your mobile  please? Mine's got no credit."

"Course," Darcy said, reaching in her pocket for her phone.

Soon it was all sorted. Sam's mum had said that if everybody wanted to go, and their parents would let them, then she didn't mind driving to Vicki's show too.

When the other girls arrived and heard about Darcy's plan, they *all* wanted to go. In all the excitement, they even forgot about Carol for a while.

Suddenly Sam remembered why they were there and interrupted her friends' excited chatter. "Right, guys," she called. "Shall we get started on our plan to find Carol?"

"Let's go!" cried Mel.

They got busy straight away. Luckily Vicki kept photographs of all her ponies on the walls in the tack room and the indoor school. She'd already given one of Carol to the police, but there were a couple of other nice clear pictures that the girls could use for their posters and leaflets.

They were going to ask Vicki if they could use the computer in her office to do them and Cara's mum had said that she'd photocopy them at work.

"Well, at the top in big letters we need something like 'Have you seen this pony?'" Jess suggested.

"Definitely," Darcy agreed. "Then, underneath, we can have one of the photos."

Vicki came in while they were sorting out the rest of the poster. She looked as if she'd hardly slept, but she asked as cheerfully as she could, "What are you so busy with?"

The girls all started to speak at once, filling her in on their good ideas for finding Carol.

"And," Darcy added, handing Vicki some paper with a phone number on it, "this is the number for my uncle Pete. He's the editor of the *Post* and he'd like to send a reporter round today so that he can get an article about Carol in this weekend's paper."

Vicki gasped with delight. "Thanks, Darcy!" she said. "Thanks, all of you. You're so sweet – what brilliant ideas!"

Sam gave Vicki a hug. "We really want to do

something to help find Carol. And somebody must have seen something."

"I hope you're right . . . I'm worried that Carol will be miles away by now though. And I've got this competition—"

"Talking of which . . ." Amber said, grinning. "Darcy's had a brilliant idea."

Vicki was really touched when the girls had filled her in on their plan for that too. "It'll be great having your support. Thanks, girls."

"We can't wait to see you in action, Vicki!" Mel told her.

"Well, don't get too excited. I'm not sure if my mind's on it now," she said. "These are gonna look great," she added, picking up one of the girls' posters. "I'll ask everybody who comes in and out of the stables – parents, vet, blacksmith, delivery guys – if they saw or heard anything unusual. And after my practice this afternoon, I'll drive round all the nearby farms and ask them too. You're right – we should be doing everything we can."

"Have you heard anything from the police, Vicki?" Cara asked.

"Just that the only clear fingerprints they got off the door and the catch to the five-bar gate were mine. I just don't know who'd do this. I mean, Carol isn't even that valuable. But she's a lovely pony and she feels special to me because we got her after Dumpling died."

The girls all felt the same, and they sat in silence, looking at each other sadly.

They were so quiet that when Henrietta and Camilla came past a couple of minutes later, the snooty livery girls didn't realize that anyone was in the tack room and carried on talking as loudly as they always did.

"I mean, it's not even like it's one of the decent ponies," Camilla was saying. "It's weird looking and *so* lazy. I don't know why everybody's so bothered."

Mel took a deep breath and clenched her fists.

Henrietta answered even more loudly, "Daddy told me that in cases like this, the ponies are hardly ever found. He thinks it's probably already been sold for meat and . . ."

The girls couldn't hear any more as the livery girls walked on past.

Cara gasped in shock at what they'd heard.

And Sam couldn't believe Henrietta could say something so horrible. "That's not true, is it, Vicki?" she asked, her voice shaking.

Vicki took a deep breath and looked Sam in the eye. "No, babe. You do hear of it in a few terrible cases, but I don't think it's likely here. Anyway," she joked, trying to lighten the mood, "Carol's too small. She's not got enough meat on her to feed a baby! Now, back to work!" she ordered. "I'll find us some sweets and we'll get these posters finished. We've got a lovely pony – and we're going to find her!"

But by the next week, Sam was starting to think that they were all wrong and that Carol would never be found. Nobody had seen anything weird on the day of the Easter egg competition and they'd had no responses to their posters or flyers.

"Any news, Vicki?" Darcy asked.

"No, honey," Vicki replied softly. "The police investigated a couple of farms nearby, but they've come up with nothing. I'm sorry," she went on with tears in her eyes, "but it really doesn't look like we're going to find Carol."

Sam couldn't believe it. "But, Vicki," she said in a wobbly voice, "I don't understand how she can have vanished. It's so weird."

"I know, babe," Vicki answered. "But let's all put on brave faces. We've just got to keep hoping that Carol's OK."

Sam knew that Vicki was right – they had to try and carry on as normal. "Come on, guys," she said. "Vicki's right. We have to get on with our jobs and stuff." And she tried to make them laugh by doing a cartwheel in the middle of the yard.

"You're right." Darcy smiled. "Come on, Sammy, or you'll hurt yourself."

"And then," Mel said with a grin, "we'll have to go to Vicki's competition tomorrow without you!"

Chapter Six

Early the next morning, Sam and her mum arrived at the stables to pick up the other girls and drive to Vicki's competition. Sam was as nervous and excited as if *she* was competing!

Darcy and her mum were already there, and so were Mel and her dad. Now that there were two cars going, there was a bit of extra space in Sam's mum's car, so Mel's dad had decided to come too – all Mel's family liked anything competitive! It was only a few minutes before Cara, Jess and Amber arrived, and they looked just as excited as Sam.

The girls piled into the two cars, giggling

and gossiping loudly. Sam and her mum
took Mel, her dad and Cara, which left
Darcy and her mum with Jess and Amber
in the other car. It was going to be a long
drive, so the girls had come prepared with
sweets and fruit for the journey, and Darcy
and Sam had brought some CDs for them to
listen to.

"Whoo-hoo!" Sam called, leaning forward
to beep her mum's horn as they pulled out of
the yard. "Here we go!"

The drive lasted a couple of hours, but it went by in a flash as the girls chatted and sang along to the music.

"OK," Sam's mum said eventually. "It's the next turning!"

"Wicked!" Sam shouted.

"Yes!" Mel and Cara called excitedly.

They gasped when they reached the car park. It was packed! There were hundreds of cars and horseboxes. And the field next door was even busier, with loads of people and horses wandering to and fro.

As they walked towards the main ring, Sam grabbed her mum's arm excitedly. "One day," she whispered, "you'll be watching me here!"

"You bet!" Her mum smiled.

"Look!" Mel called. "There's Sarah, Vicki's friend, with her husband. Don't they look different from the last time we saw them?"

Vicki had been maid of honour at their wedding and the girls had surprised them with a pony guard of honour as they came out of the church. The couple spotted the girls and Sarah waved at them.

"We said we'd meet the others by the

auction ring," Mel's dad said as the girls
waved back. "So keep an eye out for it." And
he led them across the field.

Suddenly Sam spotted somebody else she
recognized. "Mel, Car – look!" she whispered.
"There's Tim." He was with a couple of
other young men.

"Oh yes," Mel said. "I bet we see loads
of people we know here. Vicki said it's a big
yearly thing for horsy people."

"Maybe he came to watch Vicki," Cara grinned. "I think he fancies her!"

"Urgh!" Sam muttered. "I hope not. Vicki could do *so* much better!"

"I don't know why you've got such a problem with him," Mel said. "I think he's nice."

"I dunno," Sam answered, shaking her head. "I told you, it just made me feel funny that Beanz didn't like him."

Sam's mum put her hand on her daughter's shoulder and steered her to the right. "Come on, Sam, concentrate, or we'll lose you in this crowd – though maybe that's a good thing, given how cheeky you are!" she joked.

"Right, Mum, that's it," Sam retorted. "I'm hanging onto you all day just in case you try and 'lose' me on purpose!" Then she spotted the others by a nearly empty ring in the corner of the field. "Ah. The auction ring is over there," she said. Even from this distance, she could make out Jess's pink top.

"There's half an hour till Vicki's event," Darcy's mum told them when they arrived at the meeting place. "What do you want to do?"

"Let's stay here," Darcy suggested. "There are some amazing ponies being brought in for auction."

"Yes, let's watch," Sam agreed.

Darcy's mum handed round some

chocolate bars and juice cartons.

Sam was still so nervous for Vicki that she felt sick. "I think I'll save mine till later," she said.

The girls pointed out the most gorgeous ponies to each other as they sat on the grass and watched.

"Wow!" Amber cried. "Look at that New Forest pony. It's stunning."

"I'm glad Beanz isn't here," Sam giggled. "I think he'd get jealous!"

The other girls were still chatting as Darcy leaned over to Sam. "Shall we take a closer look?" she suggested. "We've still got time."

"Yay!" Sam said, jumping to her feet. "I think it's really funny that it's the person who gives the most money that gets the pony," she said as they walked over to the ring. "I mean, just look at President. He's a perfect example of why sometimes money doesn't matter. It's about how much you love them, too."

"I know," Darcy agreed. "Imagine if there were people auctions!"

"I wonder how much Henrietta and Camilla would go for!" Sam joked.

She and Darcy wandered round the edge of the holding pen. Darcy stopped to stroke a Connemara, while a bay Shetland with a white blaze trotted over to nudge Sam's tummy. The friendly pony reminded Sam of Carol and she felt tears welling in her eyes.

She stroked the little pony's nose, thinking for the millionth time how horrible the people who took Carol were.

After a while the Shetland started nosing at her pocket. Sam reached inside and pulled out the chocolate bar she'd saved. "Greedy!" she laughed, and gave a little bit to the pony, who gobbled it down immediately.

"There you are!" called Cara, coming over. "Hurry up! It's nearly time for Vicki's event."

As Sam put the rest of the bar back in her pocket, she suddenly remembered something Vicki had said just before Carol went missing: *No other pony I've ever met has liked chocolate . . . Funny*, Sam thought to herself. *Maybe all Shetlands like it.*

As Darcy caught up with them, Sam said to her, "Do all Shetlands like chocolate?"

"No," Darcy answered. "I'm sure I remember hearing that a lot of chocolate makes ponies ill. Why do you ask? Thinking about Carol again?"

"Hmmm. Sort of," Sam said thoughtfully. Something was nagging at the back of her mind, but as they made their way over to Vicki's event, she couldn't work out what it was . . .

Chapter Seven

Vicki's course looked hard! There were lots
of different types of jump, and the distance
between each one varied too.

"This is well tough!" Mel whispered.

Darcy agreed. "I'd never be able to get
round this!"

The girls cheered as Vicki and Jelly trotted
to the start. They looked amazing! Vicki was
mega-smart in a new riding jacket with her
hair in a bun under her hat, and Jelly's coat
and tack shone.

Sam was so proud of her gorgeous
teacher!

Vicki's balance and rhythm were amazing

and the girls gasped at how easily she
and Jelly took the difficult fences, instantly
adjusting to the distance between them.

The other girls cheered and commented
on how well Vicki was doing after each
jump, but Sam couldn't concentrate. She was
watching without taking it in – like when
she pretended she was doing her homework
if her mum was watching! As Vicki leaned
forward in the saddle and cleared the final
jump perfectly, everybody leaped up and
started cheering. Sam realized that Vicki had
completed the course *very* quickly, but she
was too distracted to enjoy it properly.

She was thinking hard: the friendly little
Shetland up for auction had really reminded
her of Carol – except that she was bay and
Carol was cream-coloured. But suddenly,
as the next competitor made his way to
the start, Sam remembered a mystery story
she'd read a year or so ago, and she had a

brainwave! In the book, the thief had used his horse to get away from the scene of the crime. To escape detection, he then sprayed the pony a totally different colour, turning it from chestnut to black. Sam knew it was a long shot and sounded ridiculous, but what if that had happened here? What if the little bay Shetland in the auction ring *was* Carol – *in disguise*?

"Darcy!" she whispered to her friend urgently. "Will you come back to the auction ring with me? It's really important!"

Darcy looked at her friend, concerned. Then she nodded. "Mum," she called softly, "Sam and I are going to check out the auction again now that Vicki's finished. We'll stay together and be back soon."

"OK – be careful though," her mum answered, looking over at Sam's mum to check it was all right with her. She nodded too.

"What's up, babe?" Darcy asked as soon as
they were away from the others.

"You might think I'm going mad, but . . ."
And Sam filled Darcy in on her suspicions.

Darcy gasped.
"Wow! Sounds
like a TV
mystery," she
giggled. "Maybe
they could use the
stables to film it."
But when she saw
how deadly serious Sam was, she stopped
laughing and said, "OK, let's take another
look and see if anything weird's going on."

When they reached the holding pen, it
was fuller than before and it took Sam a
minute to spot the bay Shetland. She moved
round the ring and, just as before, the little
pony trotted straight over to her and nuzzled
her as if she knew her.

Darcy smiled. "Well, she's definitely very friendly!"

"Now watch!" Sam said quietly. She took the rest of the chocolate bar from her pocket and held it out to the pony. The Shetland munched it greedily and would have eaten the wrapper if Sam hadn't pulled it away!

"Wow!" Darcy exclaimed. "That *is* weird." She rubbed her fingers hard against the Shetland's nose. "Nothing comes off. It looks like she's always been a bay."

"Well, I don't reckon they'd use normal paint," Sam said softly. "It must be, like, special pony hair dye."

"You really think it's Carol, don't you?" Darcy asked.

Sam nodded, but before she could say anything else, the auctioneer came up to them. He was a big friendly man with a red face, and he smiled kindly at Sam and Darcy.

"She's lovely, isn't she? Very gentle – a bit cheeky though!"

"Yes, sir," Darcy said politely. "Do you know where she's come from?"

"A very nice couple. They obviously loved her very much, but I think they said they were emigrating to Australia and they can't take her with them. I'm sure we'll find her a good home," he told them, and then made his way across to the ring.

Darcy shook her head. "A couple? Do you

think they're the thieves?" she whispered.

"I don't know!" Sam said. "I don't know what's going on!"

"Let's go and speak to Mel's dad before the auction actually starts," Darcy suggested.

"What if he doesn't believe us?" Sam asked.

"We'll just have to convince him!" Darcy said firmly. And she grabbed hold of Sam's hand and rushed back through the crowd to where the other girls were waiting.

Vicki was back and the girls were congratulating her. The times had just been announced – Vicki had come first!

"You were awesome!" Mel shouted.

"Totally wicked!" Jess agreed, and Cara hugged her.

Sam and Darcy ran up and started speaking at the same time.

"I think Carol's here, but she's been—" Sam started.

"There's a Shetland in the auction ring that we—" Darcy tried.

Everybody turned to look at them. Sam's mum stroked the messy red hair away from her daughter's flushed face. "There you are. I was just getting worried. What's the matter?" she asked.

Sam started again. "I know this sounds crazy, but please listen. It's really important."

"OK, honey," Vicki said softly. "We're listening."

"There's a Shetland pony in the auction ring," Sam explained. "She looks exactly the same size and height as Carol, but she's a different colour. I'm *sure* it's Carol, though, because she knew me straight away and came over. And she stuffed her face with my chocolate. Please, Vicki, please come and see her. Then you'll have to believe me," she begged.

"I do believe you," Vicki replied gently. "And I know you desperately want to find Carol. I do too, but we can't just go over and ask them to give the pony a bath so we can see if she's really a different colour. They'll think we've gone insane."

"It does sound a bit far-fetched, love," Sam's mum added.

"Mmmm," Mel's dad said thoughtfully. "It is unusual, but it's not unheard of. Let's go and check it out."

"Thank you! Thank you!" Sam gasped.

"Well," the policeman said, "if nothing else, it'll put your mind at rest."

When the group reached the auction ring, the auctioneer spotted them and came over. "Back again, girls?" he asked.

Before they could say anything, the little Shetland trotted straight over to them.

"She likes you." The man smiled and turned to Vicki. "You thinking of putting an offer in?" he asked.

"Mmmm, maybe," Vicky said thoughtfully, her eyes inspecting every inch of the pony.

"Well," the man said cheerfully, "I'll leave you to think about it."

"See!" Sam whispered. "Now watch."

"Mum, have you got any more of those chocolate bars?" Darcy asked.

"Course," her mum said, puzzled. She pulled out a bar and handed it to Sam, who unwrapped it and held out a chunk to the pony. The little Shetland gobbled it down at once.

"Wow!" Mel said. "It has to be Carol, doesn't it, Vicki?"

Vicki didn't answer, but bent down to inspect the pony's feet. "New shoes," she murmured. "Carol was only shod the day before the Easter competition."

The girls started to look excited. *Could this really be Carol?*

"Look," Mel's dad said, "I don't want to get your hopes up. This could all be a coincidence. But I'll go and speak to the auctioneer and find out some more details.

If she's up for auction, he must have her passport."

"Thank you, Daddy!" Mel gasped.

"Yes. Thank you!" exclaimed the other girls.

Vicki went off with Mel's dad. As soon as they'd left, the rest of the girls started bombarding Sam and Darcy with questions.

"What made you think her colour had been changed, Sam?" Cara asked.

"Yeah! What?" Mel asked, rubbing her hand on the pony's coat exactly as Darcy had done earlier. "Nothing comes off."

"I remembered this book my gran gave me one year for Christmas," Sam answered. "See, Mum" – she smiled – "Gran's presents are useful sometimes!"

It was only a couple of minutes before Vicki and Mel's dad returned.

"Anything?" Sam asked straight away.

Mel's dad looked unsure. "Well, there

is a passport and some documents that look legitimate, but things like that can be forged."

"I don't know Carol's registration number off by heart, so I can't check right now," Vicki added.

"Something definitely seems dodgy to me," Mel's dad told them thoughtfully. "The auctioneer reckons the previous owners are leaving the country. It's a couple who are in a real rush to sell her and only registered her for auction last week. He says they're around here today somewhere . . . I think this needs investigating properly."

"Shall we call the local police?" Vicki asked.

"No," Mel's dad said. "We don't want to make a fuss and have loads of police cars zooming up. If this is Carol – and I did say *if*, girls," he told them, "we don't want the thieves to do a runner. I'll give the station at home a call, get Carol's registration number and take it from there."

"Thanks so much, Simon," Vicki said to him. "I can't tell you how much I appreciate this. I'd kick myself if we ignored Sam and that pony *does* turn out to be Carol."

"Me too!" he said. "I wouldn't be any good at my job if I didn't check things out properly." He turned to Sam's mum. "OK, this is serious. We're in the middle of a police investigation. It's probably best if you take the girls off and wait for me somewhere else.

Why don't you have a look round the stalls?"

Sam's mum nodded. "I've got my phone with me, so call if you need anything."

"Vicki, you come with me," Mel's dad said. Then he patted Sam's shoulder. "You know, if you don't become a famous show-jumper, I'll definitely give you a job! This is excellent detective work you've done today. You're a good girl."

Sam blushed with pride. She couldn't believe how this day had turned out!

Chapter Eight

It was only five minutes before Sam's mum's phone rang. "It *is* Carol's registration number on that Shetland's passport, girls!" she said after speaking to Vicki.

"Whoo-hoo!" they shouted.

"Good one, Sam!" Mel cheered. "It *is* Carol in disguise!"

Most of the girls wandered off round the stalls with Darcy's mum, as Mel's dad had suggested, but Sam was too on edge. She went to sit down with her mum.

"Don't worry, love," her mum said. "The hard part's done now. Carol will be OK."

"I know, Mum," Sam said. "But I was just

wondering who these people are who stole Carol from Vicki."

"They're probably nothing to do with Vicki," her mum replied. "Simon – Mel's dad – seems to think that Carol could have been passed on or sold a couple of times already. That's why she's all the way out here at this auction, rather than closer to home."

"At least she doesn't look like she's been badly treated," Sam said, relieved. "She looks as happy and cheerful as ever."

"Exactly," her mum agreed. "You hear some awful things about people abusing animals. Maybe someone just stole Carol so they could make some quick cash."

After nearly an hour the other girls were back and Vicki came rushing over. "Sam, you little genius!" she cried.

"Have they caught the thief?" Sam asked excitedly.

"See for yourselves." Vicki smiled and pointed over to the far corner of the car park.

Sam could see some policeman ushering three people in handcuffs – two men and a woman – into the back of a police car.

Sam peered hard, trying to see their faces. She didn't recognize the first man or the woman, but the second man to get into the car was . . . Tim!

"No way!" Jess gasped.
"Sammy said from
the moment she met
him that she didn't
like him," Cara cried.
"And you were right,"
she told Sam.
"Who is he?" Darcy's
mum asked.

"He's a volunteer from West Farm. He
helped Vicki with our Easter competition.
Sam said there was something funny about
him then!" Mel explained. "Good one, babe!"

"It was Beanz really," Sam said modestly.
All of a sudden, she couldn't wait to get back
to the stables and see her pony. She'd spent
so much time thinking about Carol that
she'd not given him enough attention lately.
She made a promise there and then that she
was going to make it up to him as soon as
she could.

"So what's happened, Vicki?" Darcy asked.
They saw Mel's dad shake hands with one
of the police officers before making his way
over towards them.

"Well, Tim *is* genuinely interested in horses
and loves them enough to help out at Lucy's
stables every weekend – wait till I tell her
about this! – but he lost his job about a
month ago and became quite stressed about
money when he couldn't find another one."

"Oh, poor Tim," Cara said
sympathetically.

"What!" Mel shouted. "Not poor Tim,
poor *Carol*! Remember – he was there when
we found out that she was missing *and* he
pretended to be worried. What a creep!"

"You're right," agreed Jess. "He even
suggested ways to help track her down! How
could anyone do that?!"

Sam shook her head, remembering how
helpful Tim had been to Vicki.

"Surely he could've borrowed some money?" Sam's mum asked, shaking her head.

"I know," Vicki said. "It seems ridiculous, doesn't it?"

"I guess there's no way Tim could have stolen a pony from the West Farm stables because he worked there and would've come under suspicion," Amber worked out. "So our egg hunt seemed like the perfect opportunity."

"Exactly!" Mel's dad said, joining them. "You girls really would make an excellent detective squad! The competition meant the stables were so busy that nobody paid any attention to who was coming and going. Tim knew that Vicki had taken Carol over to the meadow."

"But how did he get her out?" Jess asked. "He was on the course the whole time."

"He didn't have anything to do with

actually stealing her," Mel's dad answered. "Tim texted the details of where Carol would be to his brother. Then he and his girlfriend arrived at Vicki's at the same time as all the other parents, in a car with a horsebox. It was perfect – the driveway was so full that quite a few horseboxes were left round the side of the meadow. All the other parents got out to watch, so in the middle of it they just led Carol out of the field into their horsebox. She's so gentle and friendly that she went with them without any fuss.

Then they waited until it was over and left at the same time as the parents so it looked as if they'd collected a child."

"How did they get Carol's passport though?" asked Jess.

"Tim slipped into the office once he'd given you your questions. The key to the cupboard was on the desk. 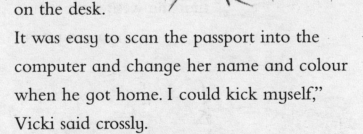 It was easy to scan the passport into the computer and change her name and colour when he got home. I could kick myself," Vicki said crossly.

"But didn't they know you'd be here today?" asked Darcy.

"No." Vicki shook her head. "Even though I mentioned the competition, I didn't say where it was in front of Tim. He must have thought they were safe because it's so far from home, and they dyed Carol's coat a totally different colour anyway."

"But then our Little Miss Detective spoiled all their plans!" Mel's dad grinned. "The local police here have arranged for one of their staff to drive Carol back home later today in a police horsebox – she'll be like a celebrity! Well done, Sam."

"I'm so proud of you, love," Sam's mum said, hugging her.

"So are we!" all her friends shouted.

"And me, babe," Vicki said softly. "You've really saved the day. Carol'll be back where she belongs tonight!"

Sam grinned proudly. Then she remembered Vicki's competition. "Oh, I'm sorry, I didn't even say well done for the competition. You were amazing, Vicki, and I'm sorry your day's been spoiled."

"Spoiled!" Vicki exclaimed. "How is it spoiled? I've got my lovely pony back thanks to you. And," she added shyly, "I'm definitely going to go back to competing properly. Today's shown me that I *can* do it."

"Wicked!" Sam shouted. And all the other girls whooped and cheered for Vicki.

"Well, it's good news all round then!" Mel's dad said cheerfully. "Now then," he said to Sam and Darcy's mums and Vicki, "shall we take these girls somewhere for dinner before we drive all the way home? It's been a very long day, and I think they deserve it, don't you?"

"Absolutely!" Vicki agreed. "I'll give your mums a call now and let them know," she said to Jess, Amber and Cara.

"Wait!" Sam shouted. "Before we go, there's one thing I want to do!" And she grabbed Vicki's hand and started to run towards the auction ring again. The other girls followed, leaving the other grown-ups looking puzzled.

Sam ran all the way up to Carol, now alone in the ring, and threw her arms round the little pony's neck.

"It's great to have you back!" she whispered.

"Careful, Sam," Vicki said with a smile.

"Why?" Sam asked.

"You might get paint on you!"

Sam laughed. "When you get home," she told Carol, "you have to have a bath!"

Darcy, Jess, Amber, Mel, Cara and Vicki all laughed too.

"Now let's go and get some dinner," Vicki said. "I'm starving."

Sam was starving too, but as she walked back to the car with her best friends, she had a big smile on her face. "I wonder if there'll be chocolate for dessert," she said.

THE END